Praise for The Hare, Raising Truth ~

"A novella about a lustful, wayward young man who finds a cursed rabbit's foot . . . The foot proves to be a peculiar version of J.R.R. Tolkien's ring of power . . . McHargue returns with an unusual tale of adolescent hormones run amok. At less than 100 pages, the book moves briskly, packed with plot and limited to a small cast of characters. The author writes from a second-person perspective . . .— a bold choice that makes the narrative more engaging . . ."

~ Kirkus Reviews

The Hare, Raising Truth

Caution: This is a naughty tale.
Keep away from children!
Disclaimer: No actual rabbits
were harmed in the creation of this tale.

Laurel McHargue

STRACK PRESS LLC   SALIDA, CO

This is a work of fiction. All characters, places, and events portrayed in this book are the product of the author's bizarre imagination. Any resemblance to actual persons, living or dead, events, or locales is entirely coincidental.

The Hare, Raising Truth

For Mike,

My lucky charm

CHAPTER 1

IT'S NOT YOUR FAULT you were born with good looks on a bad day. Not your fault your father lost control that snowy November evening, leaving you a three-year-old orphan. Not your fault your grandma's on life support in the hospital.

"Dude! What're we doing tonight?" Bucky always relies on you to come up with a plan. Has since you were in preschool together. It never dawns on him that your focus has shifted from childish games to scoring with the new girl you've been flirting with since school started in September.

"Come by after practice. Gonna do something different tonight." You slam your locker shut and catch a flash of snowy white hair down the hall. You've heard the term "albino" before, but she's the first one you've ever met. "Call you later," you tell Bucky before maneuvering through the sweaty mass of horny high schoolers. The anticipation of sitting behind Jade in AP English in three minutes gives rise to your own uncomfortable chub. You catch her before she gets to the door.

"Love sought is good, but given unsought better." The silky hair behind her ear tickles your lips.

"Wow! Someone actually read the assignment! You're a nerd, Aeron. But I'm impressed." Her voice is sweet, teasing, encouraging.

"Yeah, well, that's about the only line I remember." You slip your arm around her tiny waist and by the time she's seated in front of you, you're aching. She doesn't need to know how smart you are. It's been pretty clear from the start she likes what she sees. "Hey, heads up, it's my birthday Friday. Don't make any *girl* plans that night, okay?"

She looks over her shoulder at you, her pale green eyes affirming the answer you're hoping for. It's the first time she's really locked on to your gaze and you feel dizzy for a moment, probably because all your blood's now somewhere it shouldn't be in AP English.

Your pompous teacher stares you down from the front of the room. You're pretty sure he feels your pain. He's been flirting with Jade too. Hell, everyone's been tripping over themselves when she's around. But she's your girlfriend.

This is the first November you haven't dreaded since your parents died. Now you wish you hadn't made plans with Bucky later, but he's been your faithful friend forever. He'll get used to your new routine. It's not like you can just cut him off.

Your teacher drones on about the structure of Shakespeare's plays and when he says the word "climax," there's not a straight face in the room.

"Really, seniors?" He tries to be the adult in the room, but you know even he wishes he hadn't said the word. The bell finally ends his tedious lecture.

"Test tomorrow. Act III. Know who says what, what it means, who's keeping what from whom."

Everyone groans as they shuffle out the door to their next class. You walk with Jade, breathing her intoxicating scent, until your paths diverge.

"I told Bucky we'd do something tonight, but I'll make it up to you tomorrow, okay?" You hold her hand firmly, pulling her back to you.

"Promise?" Her doe-eyed question is full of promise.

"Promise," you tell her, and she rewards you with a timid kiss before disengaging and disappearing in the herd. Why, oh why did you make plans with Bucky? You're thankful for indoor track practice after school. You'll need to work off some adrenaline before you go hunting later.

Your mind is fixed on only one thing till the end of the school day, and when the dismissal bell finally rings, you're ready to run, to hop, to leap over whatever height the coach sets the hurdles. You run home and wolf down some cold, leftover pizza before Bucky shows up.

"Dude, how about at least changing your shirt?" He waves his hand in front of his nose. "Have you visited your grandma yet?"

"No time today. Come on. We're going hunting." You ignore the startled look in Bucky's eyes. He was expecting a junk food binge and a dirty movie, but you're feeling dangerous today. "Help me find some ammo in the garage."

"You sure that's a good idea, Aeron? I mean, who knows what's in there? Have you even opened the door since he died?" Now he looks scared, and that pisses you off, but you don't know why. Probably because you'd rather be getting it on with Jade than rooting through trash heaps trying to entertain your pal. Maybe because you feel like you've outgrown him. He's never had a girlfriend in his life. You think he's too nice. Too goody-two-shoes. Too dorky.

"Sac up, ginger. What do you think's in there? A monster? OOoooooo! Scary old garage. Come on, asshole. We're big boys now. Time to prove it."

You haven't been in the garage since you were a child, and the thought of trying to find anything in the piles of your grandfather's hoarded "treasures" makes you wonder why you ever came up with the idea of hunting, but you're also intrigued by what you might find. Perhaps the crazy old man really did collect things of value. You know there's a .22 in there. He showed you how to use it when you were about ten, and you were pretty good at hitting beer cans off tree stumps. You see it on the far wall, but it takes forever to get to it over decaying boxes of who-knows-what and around tipping stacks of musty newspapers and books.

"Is that the one your Gramps taught you how to shoot?" Bucky squints from the other side of the garage. He hasn't yet stepped into the disaster.

"Yeah, now get in here and help me find the ammo, you cross-eyed fuck. You know, maybe you'd be more helpful if you could see straight. You might even get laid. Don't they have some kind of surgery to fix that? Your parents could afford it."

You've never said anything like that to him before. You know you're being a dick. But you couldn't stop yourself. He just stares at you with his cross-eyed cross eyes, and you feel like running away. Like hugging him and begging forgiveness and running away. But you can't.

"Hey, sorry, Bucky. Uncalled for. Don't know what came over me. Just feeling like I'm missing him, that's all, I guess. I didn't mean it." You look away, guilty, because you meant it.

It's not your fault you've been on your own most of your life, your senile grandmother unable to teach you things like manners, self-respect, respect for others.

"Yeah, whatever." He kicks a box near him and it bursts open, its contents bulging from the seams. "Damn, shit smells in here. The ammo's probably near the gun. Let's get out of here." He steps over the box while you search for the ammo. He's right. It's under musty old boxes of nails at the end of the work bench.

"Found it. Let's go." You see him pushing things with his foot, waving his hand in front of his nose like he did when he showed up at your house. That pisses you off again, and you wonder what's wrong with you.

"Dude! Gross! Check this out!" Something red dangles from his fingertips, but you can't tell what it is across the dim, dusty space. "It's a nasty old rabbit's foot!" He's examining it as if he's just discovered the missing link.

You sling the .22 over your shoulder and leap over the boxes between you. By the time you get to him, you notice a strange glow in his eyes. He's about to put the foot in his pocket.

"It's mine." You grab it from him. "I remember my Gramps used to hook it to his belt when we'd go shooting. Said it would give us good luck. Looks like this has seen better days, though, right?" You slide the chain onto the snap link on your belt and try to get back on good terms with Bucky. "Don't look so butt-hurt. This thing's nasty. Take something else if you want." You push past him out the door and breathe deeply. "Whew! Let's go!"

You can't help hoping for a little luck to come your way. You know it's just a silly trinket, but hey, whatever works, right? And what was up with Bucky's eyes when he was fondling the damned thing? And, shit, why are you aroused now?

"Remember what your grandma said about talismans?" Bucky eyes the furry appendage hanging near your crotch.

"Hey, I'm up here, buddy." You point to your own eyes and shove him away. "And seriously? *Talismans?*"

"No, but really. She told us both that day when Kimber brought over her Ouiji Board that we were playing with the devil. She warned us about putting faith in stuff like that. Scared the shit out of me!"

You know better than to believe an old trinket could change your life for the better, but you slide the foot into your pocket protectively. You try not to think about how good it feels in there.

"Old people and their bogus ideas, right?" A feral black cat appears from the backside of the garage. It approaches you for the first time, sniffing the air like a dog. "Hey! Beat it!" You kick it away from you and it hisses. You won't admit it, but it freaks you out.

"It's already dark. Are you sure we should go hunting now?" Bucky looks freaked out too and you wonder this time if maybe he's right. It's been a crazy day, you have a test tomorrow, and you should probably do a little maintenance on the .22. You look at your iPhone for the time, for an excuse to call it a day.

"I guess it's probably past legal hunting time. Come on. Let's finish that old pizza and watch a Twilight Zone. I love those old black and whites."

You stare at the cat, its back still hunched, as you head to your house. What's up with *everything* today, you wonder. You lean the rifle in a corner and walk to the kitchen.

"Queue up the show and I'll nuke the pizza." While you're washing your hands you hear Bucky laughing in the living room. "What's so funny?"

"You'll never believe which episode's playing right now!" He waits for you to answer. You stick your head into the room.

"Well?"

"Episode 77, 'The Jungle'. I think this is the one with a rabbit's foot in it! Crazy, huh?"

You feel the foot in your pocket, the pressure of it making your tight pants even tighter. You squirm and retreat to the kitchen. "Yeah!" you holler. "Crazy. Be right there."

You sit far away from Bucky while watching the episode. Something makes you feel you need to protect the prize in your pocket. The pizza has never tasted better, which is ridiculous. It's a three-day-old Tombstone pepperoni. It didn't taste good the first time it was cooked. By the time the episode ends, you find yourself stroking the foot in your lap.

"Dude, get a room!" Bucky breaks your trance. Embarrassed, you throw the foot through the door into the kitchen.

"I was just trying to work off some of the grime." You know your explanation is weak and so does Bucky. "Hey, I better at least read some of this stupid play before the test, so I'll see you tomorrow. We'll hunt later this week. Oh! And I was thinking about my birthday Friday. Let's party in the cemetery like we did on Halloween! We'll plan it later. I've got some ideas and I think Jade'll come." You push him toward the door.

"Cool. Thanks for the dinner, if you can call it that, and for probably shortening my life ten years in that garage." He punches you on the shoulder and looks beyond you into the kitchen. "And you might want to remember what your grandma said about those things."

"Yeah, whatever, shut up," you tell him as you push him out the door. Bucky shrugs and opens his mouth to finish his warning, but no words come out. A flash of confusion crosses his face; he shrugs again and walks away. The stupid cat is still staring at you from the corner of the garage. If it's not gone by the time you're ready to hunt . . .

As soon as you're back in the house, you run to the kitchen and retrieve the foot. You try to look at it objectively for the first time. The fur is stiff and the whole thing smells nasty. Filling the kitchen sink with warm water and dish soap, you drop it in to let it soak. You really should study for the test tomorrow. But you know you'll ace it. You may have had shitty luck with family matters most of your life, but you were born with good looks and a good brain.

Scanning the play, you chuckle at the mistaken identities in the climax and the fact that the word climax means only one thing to, well, just about everyone. School is so lame. You're so ready to graduate and move on to . . . who knows what.

And you're so ready to get laid. Jade's crazy white hair and green eyes and juicy round ass and tiny waist are all you can think about. You slam the book closed and run to the kitchen. The water in the sink is dirty-pink, and when you fish out the foot from the bottom, the nails are flexible again and the fur feels silky-soft. Like Jade's hair. You rinse it until there's no more soap in the wet, red fur and then search in your grandma's bathroom for a hairdryer. You should probably visit your grandma soon.

When you're done, the foot is clean and soft. So strokably soft.

You'll be seventeen this Friday the 13th and you're feeling lucky, luckier than you've ever felt, which isn't saying much because of the shitty luck you've had your whole life. You'll have a killer party in the cemetery right behind your house and you won't have to worry about driving "under the influence," as they say. And you do plan to be under the influence. Someone once told you it was good luck to live near a cemetery, and now you finally believe them.

Time for bed. You take the soft, strokably soft foot under the covers with you and think about the climax in Shakespeare's—no, not that—

CHAPTER 2

YOU MAKE IT TO SCHOOL just as the second bell rings and see Jade waving to you before walking into her first period classroom. Shit! You were hoping for a kiss before the drudgery of another lame school day consumed, digested, and crapped you out. You hate it when you show up late. Everything for the rest of the day feels *off* and the sense of always being one step behind elevates your heartrate.

As if you need another reason to elevate your heartrate. What happened in your bed last night was, well, heartrate-raising, among other things. Nope. You're definitely not a little boy anymore.

In your rush to get out of the house this morning, you forgot to hide the foot in your pocket, and from the moment you walk through the door of your first hour class—tardy—you notice everyone staring at it.

"Aeron, would you please see me after class?"

You've had the hots for your history teacher since you were a freshman, but she's never given you a *look* like the look she's giving you right now.

"Ah, y-yes, Miss Hawkins," you stutter, and everyone around you giggles. They know. They've heard you talk. But you're not the only one who dreams of her at night.

Class is over before you even know what it was about, and your classmates make kissy-sounds as they leave you alone with Miss Hawkins. She leans back in her chair—suggestively, you think—and after making eye contact with you, slides her eyes down until she's staring at the fur appendage hanging from your belt loop.

"Why were you late today?" she asks, her eyes fixed on the foot, you think.

"I, ah, my grandmother, ah, it won't happen again," you stutter like a fool and wish—unbelievably wish—she'd take her eyes off your crotch. You grab a history book from a nearby desk and hold it low in front of you. "Doug forgot this. I'll bring it to him." But she knows what's up.

"If it happens again, I'll have to see you after school." Again the suggestive tone, the suggestive look in her eyes, and you wonder how any woman could be so cruel. "Now run along or you'll be late for your next class."

Never have you been so anxious to get to your next class, and as you run through the hallways, you shove the foot down into your pocket. You have no idea why it's causing such a fuss, but you don't like the attention.

Clearly, they want to take it from you. You were a fool to wear it to school. You make it to your seat before the bell rings, relieved to know you'll be able to breathe normally for the next hour as your fat, bald math teacher drills you on quadratic equations.

AP English doesn't start soon enough for you, and although you know all the answers to the test, the curve of Jade's neck distracts you. You adjust the foot in your pocket several times throughout the endless hour, and when the bell rings, you realize you've barely completed half the questions.

"What was up with that test?" you ask Jade as you walk her down the hall. "Were those trick questions or what?" You're preparing yourself for the big, red "F" you'll see on your paper tomorrow. It'll definitely hurt your average.

"No, I don't think so. Maybe instead of hanging out with that red-headed *boy*friend of yours last night you should've spent some time studying. Or with me."

"Today, after school. I'll pick you up. You can tutor me on what I obviously missed, okay? I don't have practice today." You pull her back to you and both want and fear another kiss. The distance to your next class is long, and you're already attracting unwanted attention from just about everyone.

"I have to babysit right after school, so pick me up at six and I'll try to fill you in," she says, her eyes like . . . like Miss Hawkins' eyes. "Hey, are you okay?" She hops back a pace and glances at the history book you've suddenly swung between you.

"Yes! Oh, this! Gotta run and get this to . . . to Doug, yeah, to Doug. I'll pick you up at six!" You're almost late to class. You leave the history book on someone else's desk when the bell rings at the end of the hour and run to your car, exhausted from the most stressful school day you can remember.

You wonder if maybe you should leave the foot at home when you go to visit your grandmother, but the thought of being away from it is unbearable. Besides, you'll make sure she doesn't see it. Bucky was right about one thing: she wouldn't approve of you wearing it all the time, as if it would bring you any luck. Yeah, right. You don't even really believe that. But that's probably why Gramps had to hide it in the garage. She just "couldn't abide by" such a thing. Poor Gramps. You miss the old bugger.

"Hey, Gram, how you doing today?" When you kiss her on the cheek, your lips burn. She's feverish. Not a good sign.

"Oh, you know, same ol' same ol'." She smiles with shaky, weak lips. "When are you bringing that new girl to come see me?"

"How about on my birthday? We're having a party to celebrate my last year of being a youngster. I'll bring her by before that, okay?" Talk about a real buzz-kill, you think. Better make it a quick visit before the celebration begins. But while you're thinking about your party, your grandma's face takes on a frightful expression.

"Where is it?" she asks, looking you up and down. You swallow hard.

"Where's what, Gram?" Your heart races. This isn't cool.

"You know. Where is it? Where'd you find it?" She tries to sit up, but is too weak.

"Let me get a nurse in here, Gram, you've got a fever. I'll be right back." You know you're a coward—you hate yourself for it—but you run into the hallway and grab a nurse. "Gram's burning up in there! Please give her something now, and are there lockers anywhere I can put my stuff in?"

The pretty nurse's pupils dilate when she looks at you and for a moment it's as if she hasn't heard you.

"My Gram, in there, fever, and lockers?" She points down the hall to the lockers and you push her, gently, toward your grandmother's room. As much as it pains you, you remove the foot from your pocket, put it in your jacket and store it in the locker before returning to your grandmother. By the time you get back to her, she's sound asleep. When you kiss her on the forehead, she feels cooler.

"She needs to rest now. I'll have the doctor take a look when he comes in later. I've never seen anything like that before . . . going from so feverish back to normal so quickly. Odd." The nurse leaves the room, walking past you as if you're not even there. Odd.

Time to prep for your date with Jade. With your lucky charm back on your belt, you believe you're invincible. You've never felt that way before, but today's been anything but normal. You decide it's time to really test your luck. The liquor store is a block away, and you're going to buy your first six-pack.

"Help you find something, sir?" The boy behind the counter, probably barely twenty-one, just called you "sir."

Don't blow it. Don't blow it. DON'T BLOW IT, you tell yourself as you grab the closest six-pack within reach without even looking at it.

"Ah! A rebel, you are!" he says, and you do your best to pretend you know what he's talking about, and ignore the fact that he's being a dork. "I love that website that rates beers. And I quote, 'with notes of brown bananas and green armpits, Keystone is worse than Heineken and murder!' Good choice, sir."

Yes, that's you now. A rebel.

"We don't care about what other people think, we make our own decisions now, don't we, lad." Lad? You just called him lad. Where'd that come from? But you don't care. It works, and you grab another sixer for good measure.

Brad, or Thad, or . . . Lad, whatever his name is, he doesn't even ask for your ID. He rings you up, an even ten dollars—how often does *that* happen—and you're out of there like a whore at an exorcism. You squeeze your furry good-luck charm and jump into your car, laughing out loud at what just happened and at the fact that you're driving a red VW Rabbit—a hand-me-down from good ol' Gramps. You wonder why he kept this secret from you.

You drive recklessly fast, passing more than one cruiser with cops actively digging into their bags of Dunkin Donuts, and every time you approach a traffic signal, red lights turn green before you even slow down. You're definitely going to get your buzz on before you pick up your girl. And you're definitely going to need a cold shower.

You skid to a stop in your driveway, just missing the cat. Lucky bastard jumps onto the garage door threshold and hisses as the dust kicks up in its face. But you don't have time to worry about strays. It'll move along as soon as it finds out you're not about to feed it.

The beers are cold and you down one like it was lemonade. Brown bananas and green armpits, HA! All you know is it tastes good and takes the edge off. Yes, you have the jitters. You're about to bring home the hottest girl at school. It's almost your birthday. She's into you. Pretty soon, you're going to be into her. You jerk your gherkin once . . . twice . . . three times? before jumping into the icy shower.

"Fuck!" You jump out, turn up the heat, hop back in and there you go again. It's a record. Sure, you've had girlfriends who've gone down on you before, but technically, you're still a virgin. At least that's your understanding. And this is different. Way different. You worry that you might not make it to her house by six, and that—if you do—you might not have anything left. But you needn't worry.

She's waiting for you on her front porch, all "pretty in pink"—why do girls like pink so much?—and shy-looking. You realize you don't actually know much about her, other than she's hot and smart. Better take it slow. Don't want to scare her away. You get out of your car and approach her slowly, all the while thinking about your fat, bald math teacher.

"You look pretty. How were the kids?" Talk about kids should keep your mind off your pants, off her sweet ass. For a minute, anyway, until you get back to the car.

"Oh, they're adorable. Someday I'll have my own little litter." She scrunches up her nose when she says it and for a moment, you're overcome with a desire to run away. Little litter. You suppress a gag. It's too cutsie. Too sweet. And you never really "got" kids, probably because you grew up alone with two old people.

"Whoa! Slow down, there, Nelly, this is just a study date!" You get her laughing and see her blush and you're back on track. You grab her backpack and her hand and walk her to the car, opening the door for her the way you've seen men do in old-fashioned movies. She seems to like it.

You drive cautiously, trying unsuccessfully not to sweat, and curse when you see the damned cat still in your driveway.

"Oh! Is that your cat? She's beautiful!"

And now you need to think fast. "Never seen her before. Must be a stray. How do you know it's a she?" You pray the cat doesn't hiss when you open the door for Jade. Much to your surprise and relief, it runs to her, rubbing against and between her legs. Just exactly what you hope to be doing in about an hour.

"She's sweet! Do you have any milk?" Jade bends over to pet the demon-cat and you can't seem to muster Mr. Baldy's face. Again, you need to think fast.

"Yeah, but it's old. I probably should've tossed it a few days ago, but I've been busy with my grandma and stuff. Oh, and she's really allergic to cats, so we should probably let it find another home. I'm sure someone'll feed it—her."

"Well, if she's still here when we're done studying, I'm taking her home. If that's okay with you."

Shit.

"Why wouldn't it be? Hey, come on in. I've got chips and stuff." You drop her backpack on the couch, where you plan to do a little studying. Very little studying. Your academic focus right now is on Braille Anatomy, though you plan to keep your eyes open. "Oh, and how about a brewski?" You ask as if, of course, she'd love a brewski. Like you have a brewski every day after school. Like it's what you do all the time while studying. You study her expression, which morphs quickly between surprise and surrender. It's an expression you hope to see again in about forty-five minutes.

"Sure, I think I deserve one. I didn't find any 'trick' questions on the test today. Bet I beat your score!"

"Bet everyone in the class beat my score," you say, handing her a cold one. "I don't know what happened. It's like I had a brain freeze or something." You notice Shakespeare is open to where the climax happens, and you adjust your pants, wondering whatever possessed you to shove the foot back in your pocket. For some reason, you don't want her to see it. Don't want her to freak out.

She's drinking her beer like you did earlier, but it soon becomes clear she's not experienced with alcohol. "Wow! That's some tasty brewski!" she says, and reclines on the couch in a fit of giggles. You giggle along with her and pull her back up. You've never seen any girl get so drunk so fast, but maybe it's what she wanted to do. "You don't really want to study now, do you, airy-airy-Aeron?"

Gotta think fast again. She's snuggling into you now, her hand caressing your belly, which could break an I Beam if one were to strike it right about now.

"Honestly? No. But you're driving me crazy, Jade, and I want to be sure you know what you're doing." You caress her cheek, so soft! and she lifts her face to yours, her pink lips parted ever-so-slightly. Her breath smells like fresh grass with a hint of brown banana. You kiss her, she kisses back, and you're the first to break away, dizzy.

"Nice," she whispers, and doesn't seem drunk anymore. She lands another one on you and doesn't stop you when your hand slides from her cheek to her neck to her breast to her . . . no, not there yet, back up to her sweater puppies. She moves your hand under her sweater, you have permission to go there, and works her own hand down to where you'd never say no. Suddenly, she stops.

"What's that in your pocket?" she asks, and you're about to scream, "You're kidding me, right?" but you remember what's in there. It's long past time to take it out, but you're still nervous about her reaction.

"It was my grandfather's," you explain, as if having a rabbit's foot in your pocket was somehow noble.

It's still attached to your belt, but she takes it in her hands and strokes it lovingly.

"Ooo, it's so soft," she croons, tugging on it and making you throb like you never thought possible.

"Come on, baby, don't say things like that." You slip it from her hands and push her gently back on the couch, your heart pounding in your ears and between your legs. You start to believe things just might be turning your way when there's a crash against the door. Jade screams and pushes you onto the floor and there's nothing else you can do but find out what just happened.

You open the door slowly and jump back when the freakin' cat bursts through the opening and leaps into Jade's arms.

"Oh, my God, she's shaking!" Jade cuddles the cat in her arms, and you know your study session is over. "Something must have frightened her horribly! I'm sorry, Aeron, but I think I should get home now and take this poor thing with me."

As you drive her home, a few thoughts cross your mind. First, you wonder how far she would have let you go if you hadn't been cock-blocked by the demon pussy. If only you could savor the irony, but no. You can't. Next, you wonder how you'll be able to rid the beast from your life now that it's glommed onto the only girl who's ever made you feel this . . . this studly. Finally, you wonder how in hell you're going to make it to school tomorrow after the hours of self-love you see in your immediate future. You're finally at her house.

"I had a really nice night. Thanks for letting me bring her home. I think I'll name her Salvadora. It was my nana's name, and she loved cats. Sorry your grandma can't have one . . . and that she's in the hospital." Jade leans in for a goodnight kiss, but—guess who?—sticks her evil head between you.

"Hey, I kinda told her I'd bring you to visit sometime. Is that cool?" It's about the last thing you want to do, ever, but you did tell her you would.

"Of course! I'd love to meet the woman responsible for raising such a—stimulating young man."

You walk her to her door, trying not to get caught glaring at the cat. "See you tomorrow, and don't worry about my test. I'll ask for a redo." You smile and attempt to pet the cat, but it leaps from her arms and runs into her house.

Back in your car, you squeeze your lucky charm and say, "God, let there be no school tomorrow."

CHAPTER 3

BY THE TIME YOU get back home, you're so worked up you're afraid you might hurt yourself, so you call your best friend.

"Yo, Bucky, whatcha doin?"

Hanging with Bucky generally brings you back to reality. You feel bad for him because he's always such a nice guy, and nice guys always get dumped on. His mom's really nice, but his limp-dick dad is no role model. You've always kind of wondered if maybe his dad batted for the other team, but you've never gotten that vibe from Bucky. Good thing, too, or you wouldn't have been friends for long.

"Let's go get some snacks for when we go hunting."

"When are we going? And it's kinda late, don't you think? Weren't you studying with Jade tonight?"

"Let's talk when I pick you up. Be there in fifteen, cool?"

"Yeah, sure, why not. See you soon."

Once again, you never hit a red light, and you're at Bucky's before you know it. You see him wave to his mom before leaving the house. How sweet. You recognize the real emotion you're feeling, a twinge of jealousy, but whatever. You honk your horn.

"Let's go, ginger!" You know he hates it when you call him that, but you think it's funny.

"So really, when is this *supposed* hunting trip? We don't have to go, you know, just because you found that rusty old rifle."

Yup. Good ol' good boy Bucky. Always rational. Never impulsive.

"You're kidding me, right? Listen, I know you've never shot any kind of gun before, but I'm telling you again, you need to sac up. It'll be good for you. Grow hair on your chest and maybe even get your balls to drop."

"You're a dick."

"Yeah, I know. So I dunno. Maybe tomorrow. See how the weather looks." You talk while you speed past more police cruisers and notice Bucky pressing his right foot to the floor. "Hey, take a chill pill. It's like they don't even see me today."

"Seriously? What the hell, dude?"

"I dunno. Guessing it's my lucky charm. And hey, we're covered for my party beverages already."

"No way! Who'd you sucker into buying for you this time?"

"No one. Did it myself. I'm telling you, this thing's got power. Dork at the liquor store even called me 'sir'! Do you believe that shit?" You still don't really believe it.

The supermarket parking lot is always packed this time of night with everyone coming off of shifts and mothers needing to buy one more Ding Dong for their little Johnny's lunchbox, so you're surprised when a spot opens up right by the door just as you pull in.

"Guess you won't have to dick the handicapped spot today," says Bucky, and that pisses you off again.

"Gimme a break. Have you ever, ever even seen a legit car in any of those spots? They're just there as a conspiracy to get us fat '*Mericans* to lose weight. Ha!" Bucky laughs along, but you know he judges you when you park in the marked spaces. "Hey, ever notice how close 'Mericans is to Mexicans?" The thought just dawns on you, and for some reason, you're startled, like you've discovered the cure for dorkiness.

"Again I say, you're a dick."

"What-*ever!*" You intone the word like a valley-girl and Bucky laughs—this time for real.

After loading your cart with more food than anyone could possibly consume during one day of hunting, you approach with dread the long lines of even fuller carts— carts filled with diapers and milk and burgers and butt wipes and eggs and yogurt and sodas and sanitary napkins and broccoli and bananas—at checkout. You're finally tuckered out and just want to go to bed, but the thought of bananas reminds you of the taste of Jade's mouth, and dammit if you're not hard again. Mr. Fatty-Baldy, Mr. Fatty-Baldy, Mr. Fatty-Baldy, quadratic equations, linear equations, balanced equations, dividing by pi, pi equals . . . SHIT! Pi equals pussy and how the hell are you going to get out of here without someone reporting you for pilfering sweet potatoes in your pants?

You keep the cart close, and just as you take your place behind ten other shoppers, a light goes on in the next lane over.

"I'll take you next, sir." A little finger behind the register points at you. You know it's probably dickly to cut all the others who've been waiting in line, but hey, she pointed to you, and as far as you're concerned, she's the authority.

"Damn, dude, you weren't kidding about that lucky charm," Bucky whispers. He looks like a dog with his tail between his legs as he follows you to checkout. He knows it's wrong, but it's too late now. Your bagels are already on the belt. "You're kinda creeping me out right now."

You roll your eyes at him and are happy his downer attitude has worked its magic.

You drive him home, pushing the limits of your little car, pushing Bucky's limits of self-control as you fly through intersections without even bothering to slow down anymore, and you tell him about your afternoon with Jade.

"I gotta tell you, Bucky, I've never felt boobs so soft before, except for those rock-hard nips, and her mouth—"

"Damn, dude! I really don't need to hear this." Bucky's squirming in his seat, but at least you got his mind off your speed. "Like, seriously, I don't need to hear this. She seems like a really nice girl."

You slam on the brakes and skid to a stop on a quiet street by his house.

"Holy shit, Bucky, you want her!" The realization hits you like an attack of diarrhea and feels about as bad.

"No shit, Sherlock, every dude in school wants her. And probably a few of the chicks. Exotic new girl shows up at school and you think I don't notice? Why should I be any different? It's just that you always get the girls. You've always been lucky like that. That's all. It's no big deal."

But it is a big deal to you, this confession, and you vow to make it up to him somehow.

"Hey, sorry about that. I didn't mean to 'offend' you." You make the air quotes with your fingers, a joke you've shared with him for years, and he laughs.

"No problem, 'dick-wad'." His air quotes are always better than yours. "Catch you at school tomorrow."

"Not if the great rabbit god answers my prayers!" you call out the window as he walks the rest of the way home.

You're thoughtful as you drive home. You don't speed. You're starting to get a little creeped out by the events of the day too. You hope you'll be able to sleep when you get home.

CHAPTER 4

YOU DON'T REMEMBER setting an alarm, and it takes a while for you to realize your phone is ringing. You feel as if you've been drugged. After sleeping soundly through the night, you know you should feel perky, but your head is fuzzy and you trip over your pants to get to your phone.

"Dude! No school today." Bucky's voice is cheerful and annoying. You look out your window, expecting to see a blizzard or locusts or something, but the sun is shining and the sky is clear.

"Why?" It's about all you can manage.

"Something about a frozen water line break. It'll be fixed by tomorrow, but hey, maybe this means you can finally go shoot something later." He doesn't say, "We can go hunting" or "I'm ready to sac up" or even, "You can take me hunting," and now not only do you feel like shit, but you're pissed at him again. You wonder how you've managed to stay friends after all these years.

"Yeah, sounds like a plan. I'll call you later. I should probably bring Jade with me to visit Gram today, but I'd really rather blowtorch the pubes off my balls." Hearty laughter rewards your colorful language.

"You kill me, dude."

"No, you kill *me*, ginger-balls." Another laugh and you feel the cobwebs clear from your brain.

"Later, dude. And forget what I said last night, okay? Jade's your girl. I had no business saying anything."

"Hey, you fugetaboutit." You hang up and hop in the shower. You're good for one this morning, but that's probably because you're not fully awake yet. And your lucky charm is in the bedroom.

You call Jade while pulling on your pants, your phone scrunched between your cheek and your shoulder, and by the time you're zipped, she answers with a sweet "hello?" and you wonder why she doesn't have you ID'ed on her phone yet.

"No school today! Wanna 'study' again?" She can't see your air quotes, but she gets your drift.

"I wish! No school means I've got a bunch of kids to babysit all day."

You're a clever lad. There's got to be a way around this glitch. "How about I come over and help you?" The words come out before you've had time to consider the implications. And then there's the demon cat.

"Would you? Seriously? That'd be awesome!"

"Yeah, of course. I'll bring over some snacks. Be there in about twenty." You're not sure which is worse, spending the day with Jade and her snotty charges—and cat—or spending the day with Jade at Gram's bedside. It's a lose/lose scenario whichever way you slice it. But maybe if she sees you being "good with kids," it'll pay off later.

Fortunately, the cat acts like it's afraid of the four rug snarfs and stays outside while you're there. You discover something you have in common with the cat, so maybe there's hope for you. Probably not, but just maybe.

Turns out you're the hit of the day with the kids, though, and you can only imagine it's because of the lucky charm in your pocket. There's no way you're going to let them see it. You can tell it's having the effect you'd hoped for with Jade too. You catch her looking at you appraisingly. Longingly. Mr. Fatty-Baldy, Mr. Fatty-Baldy, Mr. Fatty-Baldy. Phew. It works this time.

"Again! Again!" the kids scream, and you use them as human weights, curling them in and out with your arms, pressing them up and down with them balancing on your feet, your back on the floor.

"Coach Willie should add these to our workouts," you tell Jade, and you love to hear her laugh.

"Okay, kids, time for a snack!"

"Can the human playground get a snack too?" You crawl on all fours to where she stands and lick her leg like a dog. The snarfs howl with delight and mimic you.

"All right! All right! Enough!" She's overcome with the giggles, but you see another look in her eyes. She's

aroused. "There's enough for everyone! Now, wash your hands—twice! No cheating—and meet me in the kitchen. Her eyes lock onto yours and you're the first one into the kitchen, hands unwashed.

Without hesitation you have her against the refrigerator, your mouth hungry for more than cheesy crackers, your dirty hands acting out dirty thoughts. You're both breathless when the first snarf sneaks up behind you and pokes you in the butt.

"Hey! Not cool, little dude! Go sit at the table." You look down, and then back into Jade's dazzled eyes, and you know you won't be helping with the snacks. "I'll go find the cat," you lie, and shuffle out the kitchen door.

The cat's nowhere to be seen, and for that, you're glad. The air is brisk, perfect for a little jog around the neighborhood; it's just what you need to work off your . . . stiffness . . . from all the unusual exercises you've been doing the past couple of days.

One lap turns into three and then five, and you're finally ready to go back to the house. When you enter, you don't hear a peep. You also don't remember Jade saying anything about an outing, and before you can call her name, she steps into the kitchen with a finger to her luscious pink lips.

"Nap time. They're all asleep. We have about half an hour."

You tiptoe behind her to her bedroom, passing four little lumps in sleeping bags on the living room floor. You're conflicted about what's going to happen next.

More than ready for action, you know you won't need anything close to half an hour. Half a minute, maybe, if that. But you know girls take longer. And noise. They make noise. How are you supposed to do what you need to do without waking the snotkins?

She falls back onto her bed, pulling you on top of her, and you try to visualize a chalkboard covered in math equations—but all the equations inevitably end up equaling pi. Of course they do. You're going to need another subject. History—No! That's even worse. Miss Hawkins—No! Jade—is breathless beneath you, and you feel her hand rubbing against the lucky charm in your pocket.

"Take it out," she whispers, her voice throaty, her eyes dilated, and even though her demand could be interpreted differently, there's only one thing you're taking out.

You struggle with your belt buckle, your top button, and just as you're about to release the unbearable pressure, a child's ear-piercing scream shatters the silence and Jade kicks you away from her—such a powerful kick—and without even understanding what has happened, you're sitting against her bedroom wall with your dick in your hand, the story of your life lately.

"Aeron, come quick!" you hear Jade call to you, and you think, *Really? Seriously? You couldn't have said that about five minute ago?* But you buckle your belt back up, shake yourself off and head to the living room where you see Jade holding a child with blood running down his cheek.

"I think we need to take him to the hospital. This looks like a pretty deep scratch. Would you help the others with their jackets?"

The other kids stare at the injured boy, wide-eyed and scared. One of the crying girls says, "He grabbed the kitty too hard! She was just trying to get away! Don't hurt her, okay?"

The cat, hunched in a far corner, stares you in the eyes while you zip up jackets. *Oh, you're going down*, you think to yourself, staring right back at her.

"Don't you worry about Salvadora, honey. Let's get Mickey to the doctor so he can make him feel better."

You load up two of the snarfs in your car while Jade buckles the others into hers. Mickey is reluctant to hold a baggy of ice to his cheek, and from what you've seen, he'll probably need stitches. By the time you get to the hospital, a couple of the parents, including Mickey's, are already there. Jade must've called them on her way to the hospital. You entertain the other two kids while Jade explains what happened, and you can tell they're looking over her shoulder at you. They're blaming you. For a day that started out ripe with juicy possibilities, it's turned into a shit-storm.

When the other parents come to claim their spawn, you're ready to go home and hide in a corner. You don't see how the day could get much worse. It's only noon.

Jade walks to you slowly, she seems to read you, and stands quietly by your side.

"God, I'm so, so sorry. I just can't believe Salvadora would do that to a little boy."

But you can believe it. She didn't do it to ruin that little boy's day. She did it to ruin yours.

"I don't know much about stray cats," you lie again, "but hey, now that we're here, maybe we could stop in and see Gram." You might as well polish off a shit sandwich with piss chaser.

"That's a great idea," she says. Of course she'd think it's a great idea. You're beginning to wonder if she's looking for ways to make you suffer. You're beginning to wonder if she's worth the chase. If she's just a tease.

"She's up on the top floor. Got her an end room with a nice view of the park. Come on." You take her hand, her soft, soft hand, and soon you're halfway down the sickly-sterile-smelling hallway toward her room.

"Is that you, Morty?" you hear her call out from a distance and marvel at her hearing. Morty was your Gramps.

"No Gram, it's me, Aeron, and Jade." By the time you're in her room, she's sitting up with a smile on her face. She looks ninety-three percent better than when you last saw her.

"Ah! The lovely Jade Moon!" she says, and you know she's lost her last marble. She holds Jade's plump hand between her boney ones. It's the first time you've really noticed her claw-like appendages.

"Her last name's Bader, Gram." You kiss her on the cheek and she flushes hot again, just like the last time you kissed her.

"Well of course it is, Morty. You take me for a fool. I'm no fool. I know what you're trying to do, and I won't abide by it."

"It's Aeron, Gram. It's me, your grandson." You're embarrassed and confused by her sudden outburst. And frightened.

"It's okay, Aeron. She'll be okay soon." Jade strokes the sparse white hair on your Gram's head and she settles back into her pillows. Her smile returns. You feel like a jerk. Clearly, you're the one who upset her somehow, but you don't know what you did.

And just as you remember the rabbit's foot in your pocket, your Gram bolts back up from her pillows and points a boney finger at your crotch.

"Where is it? Take it out! Let me see it!" Her cataract-covered eyes bulge from their sharp sockets and you can't take it anymore. You bolt from the room, your heart racing, and you don't even know what to do next.

"Don't ever bring that thing in here again, Morty!—He's not the one, girlie, not the one! Keep an aspirin between your knees around that one, kitten!—You hear me, Morty? Never again!"

You hear her, all right, and you hear Jade talking to her calmly. The pretty nurse is shuffling down the hall toward you, and when Jade finally comes out to find you,

you grab her hand and bolt to the elevator. You can't breathe.

"Let's get the hell out of here," you say when you're in the elevator. "I don't think I can do this anymore." Maybe you mean you can't visit the hospital again. Maybe you mean you can't be with Jade anymore. You just don't know what you mean. You just know you're ready for this day to end.

But by the time you're back in your car, you think perhaps there's a way to salvage the day. You've had nothing but good luck when you've gone to the store lately. What would make you think anything would be different now?

"I guess it's my turn to apologize," you say. "God, I don't know what just happened in there, but they told me this could happen. I just didn't think it would happen so quickly." You're looking for a little sympathy and it's working. She leans over and puts her hand on your leg. Its warmth penetrates your jeans. "Do you think that kid—Mickey?—will be all right?" Your interest in the kid is insincere, but you know how much she loves her practice "litter." You feel dirty, and not in a good way.

"Let's see. His mom just texted me." Jade's pretty brow furrows as she reads the text. "Unbelievable. She said it's a miracle. When the doctor came in to stitch his cheek, he couldn't even find where the cut was. I think we lucked out on that one, huh?"

Lucked out. You're not sure who lucked out today, but it doesn't feel like you.

"Then it's a good time to buy some scratch-offs, I'd say. Let's stop by the gas station before I take you home and pick some up. I might get a few more things for my party Friday night too. You're coming, right?"

"Of course I'm coming. Why wouldn't I?"

"Just making sure." You open her door when you get to the gas station and whisper in her ear, "Watch this. And just act like everything's cool." You grab a case of beer and walk to the snack aisle. Jade looks at you like you're insane, but you give her a "be cool" reminder look. "And I'll take five of the dollar scratch-offs."

The guy behind the counter rings you up without incident, but you can tell there's something bothering him. A chubby, greasy-haired man of about thirty-five—you're not good at judging age—he's looking at you and he's looking at Jade, and he's looking at you again and then back at Jade. You don't like the way he's looking at Jade. He takes off his gas station cap and scratches his head.

"Hey, you got a problem, pal?" You have your bags, you have your scratch-offs, you should just turn and leave. You've had more than enough drama for one day, but this guy's getting on your last nerve.

"As a matter of fact, I do," he says, and Jade gives you a "let's get out of here" nod toward the door. "How is it a dude like you scores a babe like her?"

"It's none of your business, fuck-face," Jade says. She grabs you by the belt and pulls you toward the door. You're startled and amused and you start to laugh. You've never heard her talk like that before.

"Yeah, it's none of your business, fuck-face. Why don't you do humanity a favor and drop dead." You're out the door before he gets out from behind the counter, and you're pretty sure he can't leave the store unsupervised. Some other customers are still standing there. One of them probably recorded the interaction.

"That was kick-ass," you say to Jade, and she kisses you. You're both pumped on adrenaline.

"I know, right? How'd you pull that off? You're not even close to legal! I hope I didn't embarrass you, but that guy was a jerk."

"I think you mean a fuck-face, and no, you didn't embarrass me." You laugh together and wish you could start the day all over again. When you're almost back to her car at the hospital, you tell her, "Listen, I kinda promised Bucky I'd take him hunting later on, so I hope you don't mind if I drop you off now."

"Hunting? You mean as in killing-animals-hunting?" Her laughter stops.

Shit.

"Well, Bucky hasn't . . . and I don't usually . . . mostly just target practice in the woods . . .," but it's too late. The rabbit's out of the hat. She knows you're an animal killer now. And suddenly, the thought of doing anything else today feels overwhelming. All you really want to do right now is go home and go to sleep.

"Let's just call it a day, okay?" you ask in your most charming voice. "It's been a rough one. I'll tell Bucky no-can-do tonight. Let me take you out to dinner tomorrow night and we'll make it a real date. No kids. No crazy cats. No crazier grandmothers. Just us. Sound good?" She looks as tired as you feel.

"Sounds good. I just . . . I'm just not crazy about the hunting idea, okay? So let's not talk about it. Deal?"

"Deal. Hey, maybe we'll get another day off tomorrow. But if we do, don't call me until the snarfs are gone. Deal?"

"Deal."

You pull up next to her car and give her the scratch-offs. She gives you a chaste kiss. You call Bucky on your way home and cancel your hunting plans, which you know makes his day. It's still light out when you hit the sack, but you don't care. You're a rebel. A dead-tired rebel. You're asleep before you hit the pillow.

* * *

Back at the gas station, a crowd gathers around an ambulance at the store. You didn't see fuck-face gripping his chest right after you left.

CHAPTER 5

BUCKY'S CALL WAKES YOU from a dead sleep for the second day in a row with the same news.

"I don't know how you're doing it, dude, but this is unbelievable! Two days off! SWEET!" His boisterousness gets under your skin. "What happened to you yesterday?"

You're finding yesterday's events hard to believe too.

"Meh, I dunno. Don't really want to talk about it. I think I might be getting sick."

It's not a lie. You're definitely off your game. Lethargic. Drained. Still, it looks like another beautiful day, and since you're not about to go near Jade's snarfapalooza—you're taking her out for a nice dinner tonight—you decide a day in the woods is just what you need. Clear your senses. Put some pep back in your step.

"Let me get some breakfast and a shower and I'll pick you up in forty-five. Time for you to 'kill the Wabbit,'

Buckaroo." You do your best Looney Toons impression, but you know your buddy's hesitant.

When you turn on the news, you're frightened by the sound of your own voice.

". . . humanity a favor and drop dead . . . ."

"What the—" Your heart races, you're fully awake, you're in a nightmare, you've been caught, you're going to jail, you're fucked.

"Timothy Smith, longtime employee of the local Kum & Go, dead at twenty-seven. Coroner reports a genetic heart disorder, but anyone with information about the man in this video, please call your local Police Department."

You stand transfixed as an amateur video—probably shot by one of the bystanders in the store—shows you holding a case of Keystone and heading out the door. Fortunately, the image is a blur, and even you'd have trouble positively ID'ing yourself in a lineup. It's definitely your voice, though, telling the lecherous schmuck to drop dead.

But wait! Where's Jade? Wasn't she pulling you out the door? Did she leave the store before you told that fuck-face to drop dead? You can't remember. She must have been out the door before the customer got out his phone. Strange that the store's video surveillance didn't catch the whole thing, but maybe when ol' Timmy decided to hit on your girl, he turned off a switch or something. They said it was a genetic thing, his heart condition, but still, you glance at the rabbit foot attached to your pants on the floor.

You turn off the news, toast a bagel, slam back a glass of O.J. and start to feel a little better. As long as Jade doesn't say anything to anyone, you're safe. You're surprised you haven't heard from her yet with news of winning the Jackpot on the scratch-offs you bought for her. Probably saving her demonstration of appreciation for after dinner tonight. Maybe you'll get extra lucky and she'll pick up the tab. You finally feel a rise down below thinking about just how she's going to thank you. Sure, you have time for a quick one in the shower.

After dressing—you really should wash those jeans soon—you load up the hunting gear and treats and head to Bucky's. You turn off the radio when you hear your voice and Timothy's name again. It's your voice, you know that, but the sound—like the image on TV—is distorted. You squeeze your lucky charm and tell yourself it wasn't your fault. How could you have known the guy had a bad ticker? You couldn't. And besides, he was a creep. He did humanity a favor.

You see Bucky kiss his mom goodbye when you pull up to his house and wonder what it would be like to have someone healthy and supportive taking care of you at home. It feels like you've had to be the caregiver for most of your life. Not fair, you think. But then again, you're the one getting lucky tonight. You can feel it. It's time. No more pussyfooting around, as they say.

"Let's go, bro! Today's your lucky day! We got ammo, we got food, we got beer, we got a forest full of furry meat just waiting to hop into a stew, what more

could a man want?" Well, you know what more you want, but you'll get that later.

"Beer? Are you kidding me? In the middle of the day? Is that such a good idea . . . I mean, with a gun and all?"

"God, Bucky! Can you for once stop being such a buzz-kill? It's a fuckin' .22, we have a fuckin' excellent day off, you're gonna get fuckin' drunk and shoot a fuckin' rabbit. Got it? Trust me, it's gonna change your life."

"Fine, dude, whatever." You see him nod his head as if trying to convince himself you're right. Of course you're right. "Okay. I'm ready. Let's do this."

"We're gonna do this. We're *doing* this." Finally! You think he might finally man up. You park at the trailhead and distribute the gear and food between you. "I'll carry the .22 until we get to a spot where Gramps and I used to hunt. There's no way you're not gonna get something today. It's about half a mile in. You ready?"

"Ready. You'll show me what to do when we get there?"

"No, duh! I'm just gonna hand you the rifle and say go for it. Of course I'm gonna show you what to do. Now here, drink this. It'll take away the jitters. You don't want the jitters when you're aiming."

He's committed to doing what you tell him to do today. You can see it in his face. His eyes squint while he chugs the beer and you remember the website description good ol' Lad shared with you—brown bananas and green armpits—but you don't want to think about the grassy-banana taste of Jade's sweet mouth right now, so what was that other part? Oh yeah, "worse than Heineken and murder." How appropriate, you think.

Bucky's smiling by the time you set up behind Gramps' favorite downed tree. You try not to let it bother you that he picked up your empty can after you dropped it next to the trail. Such a goody-two-shoes, even with a buzz on. But the old thrill of the hunt soon rushes through your veins and your senses tingle. Time for silence.

"Now, watch how I do this, okay?" you whisper, and Bucky nods. "Pay attention. And get that goofy grin off your face." You rest the forestock in your left hand, your left arm supported by the tree, and show him where you press your cheek for the best aim. "Try to keep both your eyes open. You'll see the crosshairs in the scope come into focus just fine with your right eye. I think." It dawns on you that you don't know how someone with crossed eyes sees. "If that messes you up, just close your left eye and you should be fine. Here." You hand him the rifle and jostle him as noiselessly as you can into position. Well, as close as you can. He's definitely not a natural.

"If I close my left eye I can see the crosshairs okay."

"Keep your voice down, dorkenheimer. That's good. I'm gonna slide in the magazine and show you how to load a round now. Lift this handle and pull back the bolt. Good. Now slide it forward and down. Good. Hey, keep your finger off the trigger until you're ready to fire! Don't you know anything about guns?" You know he knows nothing about guns.

"Now what do I do," he whispers. You've never seen anyone more uncomfortable-looking than he looks right now.

"Now you wait and look around. You stay alert to movement. And when you see movement, it'll probably be a squirrel or groundhog or rabbit, look through the scope and put the crosshairs on it. If you get that far, *then* just move your finger to the trigger and squeeze. Easy as pie." Dammit. Why do you keep coming back to that tasty dessert you plan to have in your face tonight?

The two of you sit quietly for a while, both of you scanning the forest floor, and then it hits you.

"Hey, I need to take a dump. You stay here. If you see something, go for it. Be right back."

You move away behind Bucky and find a boulder to squat behind. You dig a little ditch and drop your pants. You're amazed by what lands in the hole and hurry back to where Bucky still crouches uncomfortably.

"Holy shit, Bucky, and I mean that literally! I almost didn't cover it up!" You wish you'd brought your iPhone. "I just pinched off a foot-long *clean!* I've never seen anything like it!"

"You're disgusting."

"I know, but seriously! You should've seen it! We're talkin' Guinness Book of World Records here!" You're having a hard time controlling your volume. "I know, I know what you said about this rabbit's foot, but I'm serious. I'm keeping this thing forever." You really want to tell him about how confident you feel that you'll be going all the way with Jade tonight, but you remember his reaction the last time you shared your "exotic new girl" exploits.

You hear a rustle in the leaves beyond your concealment.

"Shhh! There she is, eleven o'clock about twenty feet!" A fat old rabbit sits there munching on long blades of grass, oblivious to the danger just a stone's throw away. It takes everything in your power to keep from grabbing the rifle from Bucky, who squirms into position. He's making too much noise and the rabbit stops chewing for a moment, looks to the right and the left, hops a few feet, and settles back down.

"Stop thrashing around, dork, you're gonna scare her away." Your whisper is harsh. Bucky stops moving. You see him squinting at the scope, his finger moving slowly from the trigger guard to the trigger, and you anticipate the bang.

PING!

An old beer can sails into the air and you watch the rabbit disappear like a shot.

Bucky sits up and rests the rifle against the log. He looks like a scared little boy.

"Sorry, dude, I just couldn't do it. She was sitting there all cute and innocent . . . I just couldn't do it." He looks away from you.

He's never let you down before, and although you're pissed off—the rabbit was probably about to die soon anyway—you understand what he's telling you. You'll never let him know how long you cried after your first kill, but every time after that got easier.

"Hey, take a chill pill, ginger. Sweet shot at that beer can, though! I'm pretty sure you'll have no trouble getting a clean shot at a *real* target when you're finally ready to sac up." You punch him on the arm to let him know you're still cool, and he looks back over his shoulder into the trees. You wonder if he regrets missing his perfect opportunity, and then you remember something someone told you about rabbit's feet.

"Maybe this Friday at my party! Supposedly, rabbits killed in a cemetery on a Friday the 13th by a cross-eyed redhead fuck are the ones that end up as actual lucky charms!"

"You are seriously the biggest dick I know, and I said *are,* not *have*." He sounds irritated by your suggestion, but you can tell he's thinking about it. Considering it. Maybe all he needed to do today was prove to himself he could aim at something and hit it.

"Don't worry about it anymore. Let's get outta here." You fire off a few practice shots at tree limbs before unloading the weapon, and then you get another idea. "I'm leaving this with you until my party. Go ahead and practice with it in your backyard, set up some cans along your fence or whatever, and just get comfortable with it so you're not all flouncing around and scaring shit away when it's time." And then that look of concern clouds his face again. "What? What's wrong now?"

"Well, my mom, you know, and my dad—"

"Yeah, I should have guessed it. You're still mommy and daddy's perfect little boy. Silly me to think you'd ever have the courage to man up around them. Ever." You know you've gone too far as soon as the words are out, but it's too late.

"Gimme that thing, fuck-face," he says, and grabs the rifle from your hands.

"What did you just call me?" You feel like you've just been punched in the gut.

"Fuck-face. What about it?" he asks, matter-of-factly.

"Did you see the news this morning?" If anyone could ID you from the Kum & Go report, Bucky could.

"No. Why?"

"No reason. Some guy had a heart attack at the gas station yesterday and some jerk in the background called him a fuck-face, that's all, so when you just called me that, I kinda got 'offended.'" You hope your little confession and the air quotes will get you back on track and keep him from searching out the report.

"Fine. I'll remember you only want to be called 'dick-wad' from now on. How's that?"

"Fine. Let's roll." You see rabbits everywhere on your hike back to the car.

Bucky takes the weapon with him when you drop him off. You made sure he knew how to load and unload it before you put it back in its bag, and he laughed when you suggested he might wait until his mom goes shopping before doing any target practice in her vegetable garden.

It's only two p.m., but you're exhausted. There's no way you're going to get sick before your birthday, though, so you wolf down a cold cheese sandwich back at home, hop into bed and spank your monkey before napping in preparation for your lucky night.

CHAPTER 6

ONE LOOK AT JADE when you pick her up at her house and your dick could split a diamond. You're glad you wore the only suit jacket you own because your Gram bought it for you last month "just a tad too long" so you could grow into it, and boy, are you growing into it right now.

"Wow. Wow." You stop yourself from saying it again, but wow. You try not to stare at her lady lumps pushing the limits of her white cashmere sweater, but, come on. Why would she wear something like that if she didn't want you to stare? You're pretty sure she's not even wearing a bra, and the effect is stunning.

"Oh! Just a minute," she places her hand on your chest, "I forgot to put out Sal's kibble."

Sal. Salt. Salted, sautéed kitty. You can't believe someone didn't make Jade put down the damned cat after it attacked that kid, and wonder if your lucky charm somehow protected it that day as well. Bummer of an idea. At least you're ready to walk Jade to the car now when she returns.

You open the car door for her—ever the gentleman!—and catch your breath when she lifts her legs into the car. You can't imagine she doesn't know what she's doing to you. It's impossible not to get a quick glimpse of what must be her softest parts because she's not wearing any panties either, and since the rug matches the curtains, it makes a statement against her short, dark skirt.

"Everything okay?" you hear her ask, and realize you're still just standing there holding the door, staring at her legs.

"Yes! Yeah, I just wanted to make sure you're all in." You close the door and run around to your side, glad, once more, for Gram's gift of the oversized jacket. Just the thought of Gram tonight will keep you in check. You hope.

"I'm starving!" she says. "I haven't eaten anything today because of what you said about the food at this restaurant. I have a feeling I'm going to stuff myself tonight. Just a warning!" She laughs. Why do you translate everything she says into a double entendre? Must be all that Shakespeare you've been reading lately.

"Trust me, I wasn't kidding about it. So, hey, tell me, how much are we looking at on the scratch-offs?" You were planning to wait for her to tell you the good news when the tab came after dinner, but now you just want everything between now and dessert over quickly. You're a little worried about a growing sense of unease plaguing you since you went hunting. Probably just residual adrenaline, but now it's making you jumpy.

"Oh, those. Ha! Well, I'll give you your five bucks back if you'd like, because that's what I got. At least that's kind of lucky, right?"

But kind-of-sort-of-almost lucky isn't what you want tonight. You're shooting for all-in lucky. She better love her meal.

"Would you like to see a wine list, sir?" the waiter asks. Good. It's still working.

"Why don't you bring us a bottle of your Sommelier's Choice," you tell him. You looked it up on the interwebs before picking up Jade. The look of approval in his eyes as he bows, ever so slightly, makes you feel like you're the king of the hill. The cock of the walk. And even though you were hoping for a big win with the lottery tickets, you have a credit card Gram gave you "for emergencies."

You do the swirly thing with the splash of wine in the glass, give it a sniff and swallow, like you've seen in those old movies. It's good.

"Is the lady ready to order?"

You're not sure if you should order for her, but you realize once more how little you know about her, other than her heat index. You give her a nod.

"Yes, please, I'd like the vegetarian quinoa dish with a side of baked turnip."

You're kidding me, you think. The place is known for its filet mignon and lobster, which is what you order, and she orders the diet dishes. You just don't get girls and their weird habits, but she ordered the cheapest things on the menu, so that's lucky for you. If you ordered something like that, you'd be farting all night, and while you might think it's funny, she probably wouldn't agree. And you're not even close to feeling like you could let one rip when she's around. You wonder about how that stuff affects girls, but shake the thought from your head.

Jade's already relaxed and glowing with half a glass of wine when the meal is presented, and you're impressed by her girlie meal.

"You want a little nibble, don't you," she teases you, circling a forkful of fluffy stuff in front of your lips. You devour the stuff like an eagle plucking an unsuspecting mouse from the ground, and it's not bad. She laughs and surveys your plate.

"I suppose you wish you had my meat," you say, which is not how you meant to say it, but it's out there, and you're amazed she doesn't seem to pick up on your gaffe.

"No, not really," she says, "but I'd like to try some of your cheesy broccoli!"

Girls and their veggies. Cheese or no cheese, you weren't going to touch the stuff, so you load up your fork.

She grasps your outstretched hand between hers, and looking you deep in the eyes, licks her upper lip before drawing your offering into her open mouth. She clamps her lips together and slowly, so slowly, draws the fork out empty.

"Mmmmm," she moans.

You catch yourself before a puddle of drool breaches the brim of your lower lip. Maybe you just might try the stuff after all.

You don't even notice the waiter when he returns to your table. He clears his throat.

"Will there be dessert?" he asks.

You want your dessert *now*, right now, under this table or hell, on it, but you see Jade take the dessert menu from him.

"I'll have the carrot cake, please," she tells him.

"Just coffee for me, please." You don't want any lingering side effects from the wine later.

When the tab finally comes, you notice they forgot to charge you for the wine, the lobster, the extra sides and the dessert. You could pay the total with cash, an even thirty dollars, but you put in your credit card instead. No need to let Jade know about their mistake, and you'll be sure to leave a nice tip.

Back in the car with another flash of muff—so white!—you speed to a special make-out spot only you know about. It's going to happen. It's finally going to happen.

Without a word when you turn off the ignition, she's on your lap and you're lip-locked. Moments later you're at second base with no warnings, and even if you could get your hand up her sweater, you don't need to because the soft fullness of her breasts is only enhanced by the tight softness of her sweater. The sensation makes you dizzy, and you fear the wine was more potent than you thought.

But no, there's no need to worry about being able to perform tonight. You go for the kill slowly, your hand sliding imperceptibly up her inner thigh while you try to control the brain in your pants that's telling you to *heave, HO!*—and when your fingertips burn with her heat and you know you're just about to feel the tickle of her soft white patch she pulls away, panting, and holds your face between her hands.

"You know I have to wait till I know it's right, right?"

Wrong. Wrong-wrong-WRONG! You know no such thing.

"Oh, come on, baby, you know you want this. You know it's right. It's almost my birthday and I just took you for the best dinner you've ever had and oh, my, GOD, you're not wearing any underwear. What do you think that tells a guy? What am I supposed to think? I love you, you wild thing, and I want you. I want you bad."

It's dark, but you see something glisten in the corner of her eye.

"If you loved me, you'd wait. You'd wait until I knew for sure it was right. You'd wait as long as I needed. Why can't we just make out?"

"Because, well, see? I'm in a lot of pain right now, and remember when you told me yesterday to take it out? What's changed between then and now?" You don't want to make her cry, but even you're starting to worry that being hard for so long without relief might be harmful to your health.

"I wanted you to take that rabbit's foot out of your pocket. Some sharp things in it were poking me."

"Damn, girl! There you go again! You're always saying and doing things that make me think you're ready to do it. Our little interrupted 'nap' time, the way you dress—you know how easy it is to see up your skirt?—that fork foreplay in the restaurant, talk about poking you . . . you're driving me crazy."

"Hey, you don't even know who I am. You just think I'm a piece of hot snatch. And I'm sorry if what I'm willing to give you just isn't enough, but I think you should take me home now." She uncrosses her arms and slides over to fasten her seatbelt.

"You're right, I don't know who you are, but I want to." You drive her home in silence and leave the engine running in her driveway. "Hey, let's not do this. Come here, wildling." You kiss her gently. "We'll talk tomorrow, okay? Just talk." You don't get out to open her door. You've been tortured enough for one night.

When she's in her house, you race toward Bucky's, calling him on the way.

"Bucky! Buck-buck-buckaroo! Come on, pick up, pick up, PICK UP!"

"Dude, what is wrong with you? It's ten o'clock! You know everyone here's already asleep."

"You gotta go out with me, Bucko, I'm serious. Put on your clothes. We're going to Foxy's."

"Are you outta your mind? No way we're getting in there. And even if we could, you know we're back to school tomorrow."

"Pulling into your driveway now. Find your balls and let's go."

"Fuck, dude, give me a couple minutes. And go park down the street. I'll be right there."

Ten minutes later you see him in your rearview mirror. He actually put on some nice clothes.

"Thought you and your lady were spending some quality time together tonight," he says when he's buckled in.

"Yeah, we did. And now it's time for you to have a little fun too." You've heard Foxy's is the place to go if you want to get laid, and as much as you want it to be with your girl, you're not about to wait until . . . whenever. You're pumped from the thrill of hunting and the anticipation of thrusting your way into that silky white patch and you just can't stand it any longer.

The place is hopping when you and Bucky walk through the door—you hoped your lucky charm still worked on other people and it did—and soon you're grinding on the dance floor with drunk girls of every size and age. You laugh at Bucky, who appears to be following the gyrations of people around him and occasionally mimicking you. Not bad, you think. Boy can move.

A particularly attractive brunette, obviously a wig, locks eyes with you and works her way through the glistening bodies to dance with you. You can't judge her age—never could with anyone—but even though you suspect she's older than she looks, she's smokin' hot. Her red satin dress leaves little to the imagination, and your imagination has her dress up over her hips and her ankles digging into your shoulder as you drive her hard and deep right there on the dance floor.

"Oh, *really*," she says when she reaches you, and you wonder if your thoughts are that obvious on your face. But she's looking at the bulge in your pants, and you don't even try to hide it anymore. She reaches behind you and grabs your ass, working you down to a slower rhythm, and when she nibbles your earlobe, chills run down your spine and you have to remind yourself to breathe.

As much as the thought kills you, you know this would be the perfect time to show your loyalty to your friend. Once you know he's good to go, you'll treat yourself. You've never done this before, so you just straight-out ask.

"Hey, ah, see my friend right behind me? The ginger with the moves? Do you think you might, you know, make him a man tonight? I'll pay whatever you ask."

She squeezes your ass and steps back just enough to keep brushing against your rock-hard wood in time with each drop of a beat.

"Your friend, huh? And here I thought you wanted me, big guy."

You wonder what the hell you're doing.

"Sure, I'll take him. What's his name?" She laughs when you tell her his name and you turn as she glides around you and takes his hand. He looks startled and pleased, his goofy grin one only his mother could love.

You try to pretend you're not paying any attention, but the music is slow now and you hear her say, "So, new boy, what do you say we take this dance upstairs? You feeling lucky, Bucky?"

Pleased with yourself, but jealous of your friend— he's gonna seriously owe you for this—you scan the room for someone as hot as scarlet-dress-woman, but none can compare. You look around for second best when you feel a hand on your ass again. You turn around right into the breast of a scarlet dress and see Bucky over her shoulder giving you the "not for me" sign.

"That baby's not ready for me to burst his bubble, boy, but you are. Let's go."

You justify your decision by telling yourself it would be a waste to let a fine piece of tail get away. Besides, the woman is insistent.

You look back at Bucky as scarlet-dress-woman pulls you by the belt toward the stairs. He gives you a weak thumbs-up and disappears in the crowd of dancers. It's not your fault he'll be a virgin till he's fifty. You did your best. You did more than your best.

You honestly cannot believe what's happening right now, but you couldn't have asked for a better ending to your day. Your week. Your life. You could probably die right now a happy man. Well, not right now. Maybe in about ten minutes. Or five.

The room is small but who cares. You have no idea what to say, how to proceed, or what this will cost, but you don't give a shit about any of that either. She throws her purse on a desk and looks at you with pale blue eyes, paler than Jade's green ones. But you don't want to think about Jade right now.

"So, tell me *your* name, Bucky's big, generous, generously endowed friend."

It takes you a moment to remember your name, probably because there's very little blood left in your brain.

"Ahh, Aeron. Um, you look really beautiful tonight. Stunning, really. I love your dress." You're a moron. *I love your dress . . . stunning, really . . .* what do you think you are, a fashion design agent?

"You like my dress, huh?' she says, and as you nod your head like an idiot, she walks toward you, slowly, her full hips swaying hypnotically, and slides her dress up inch by inch until she's standing right in front of you. She tugs on your belt again and rubs her other hand up and down against your straining manhood and no math equation, history lesson, track coach or science experiment can bring you back down.

"What's this?" she breathes into your ear and you know she's found the rabbit's foot.

"Nothing! Nothing, really, just an old thing I found somewhere." You reluctantly push her hands away and fumble your way out of your pants, letting them drop to your ankles. You're glad you put on a new pair of briefs.

"Nice. Very nice," she says. She kneels in front of you and nibbles your belly gently as she slides down the only thing left between you and her mouth. Ever so lightly she licks the length of your shaft and your legs tremble.

"I . . . I . . ." your breathing is shallow and you're afraid you might fall.

"Aye aye, Captain!" she says, and at any other moment you'd laugh, but not now.

She sits back on her heals, releases the clasp behind her neck, and pulls you to your knees. She looks down at her voluptuous breasts and then back at you, waiting for you to reach out and caress them. Your hands tremble as you touch them. Your whole body trembles.

Just when you think you can't take another moment of throbbing anticipation, she reclines on the floor in front of you, what's left of her scarlet dress hiked up over her hips, her long legs spread to expose engorged pink lips beneath a small white patch of fur.

"Do whatever you want with me, big boy. Cherries are on the house tonight."

* * *

An hour later even she can't believe how many times you were able to come, and you're pretty sure she eventually didn't fake it either.

You're at the door, Bucky's probably pissed by now but he'll get over it, and you're not sure what to say when you leave.

"So, ah, I had a really good time tonight. Thank you. Really, thank you."

She looks at you with sleepy eyes from the bed and smiles. She looks older than she did with her dress on.

"What's your name?" You feel like a jerk for not asking her earlier.

"Just call me Bunny."

CHAPTER 7

EVEN THOUGH YOU PRAY for another day off, school is back in session. You haven't cracked open a book in days, you know you're behind in every subject, but you don't care. You slept like the dead last night. And you're a man now. You're pleasantly sore all over.

You leave your nice pants on the floor, the rabbit's foot still in a pocket, and pull on your jeans. You don't bother to put it in your pocket today because you're a new person. You don't need that stupid lucky charm anymore.

But you get a bad vibe as soon as you pull into the school parking lot. Everyone looks at you sideways and walks away when you get near them. They murmur to one another and giggle.

Bucky's at your locker when you get there.

"Dude, I have no idea how, but I think Jade found out about last night. She's not in school today—Pam said she has cramps or something—and everyone's pissed at you."

"What do you mean, everyone's pissed at me? Why should anyone be pissed at me, except maybe you, you virgin ginger. Hey, that's a great name for a drink, a virgin ginger!" But Bucky doesn't laugh.

"I'm serious, dick-wad. They're all saying you walked out on the best thing that's ever come your way. And she's really hurt."

"Well, how'd she find out anyway? I know you'd never tell her, would you?" You hate that you're not sure.

"You know, I really hate you sometimes." Bucky shakes his head and you feel like an asshole.

The bell rings and you're almost late to class again. No one talks to you, but you hear snippets of snide remarks about "the birthday boy" getting lucky last night. You can't imagine anyone from the club would've known you from school. You had to be twenty-one to get in unless you were with the lucky-charm-boy.

And now you get the feeling your party isn't going to be the party you expected. Who cares, though? You had a night last night that tops any party any high school dork could've imagined.

You wish you didn't care.

The day never ends, and after track practice—you nearly kill yourself on one of the first hurdles—you're stopped on your way home by a cop who probably hasn't seen his own dick in decades.

"Do you know how fast you were driving, sonny?" He has powdered sugar on his chin.

"Gee, no, officer. I'm on my way to the hospital to visit my Gram. She's pretty sick, and I guess maybe I was just thinking about getting there before she, well, you know . . ."

It works and you get by with a warning, but shit! Why'd you leave the foot at home? You feel just a little guilty using your Gram as an excuse, but hey, what she doesn't know won't hurt her. If you're honest with yourself, you've already said your goodbyes, back before she went Looney Toons on you.

You throw your backpack on the couch, grab a Keystone from the fridge and slam it. Why are you so tired? Oh, yeah, you had a bone-a-thon last night with a sexy little "Bunny." Bizarre. Hot. Fantastic. She made you suffer, but God Almighty, did you love it.

Huh. Just the thought of one minute from last night, one second, should make you hard by now, but . . . nothing. Must be the beer. The fatigue. You'll take a hot shower and by the time you get your lather on, Old Faithful will be primed for eruption. But when you walk into your bedroom, you scream like a little girl.

"Shit, Jade, where'd you come from?" You see her standing over your dress pants, her arms folded across her breasts as if protecting them from lurking wild animals.

"Tell me the truth, Aeron. Did you really do it? Did you really leave me last night just to go score at the club with Bucky?"

"Did Bucky tell—"

"NO, you jerk, Bucky didn't tell me anything. He'd never snitch on his best friend. But you don't know what it means to be a best friend, do you. And you sure as hell don't know how to be a boyfriend. Just because you don't have any other friends in town doesn't mean I haven't made a few since September."

Ooo. That stings you.

"Jade, come on, let me explain—"

"Explain WHAT? Explain how you used this horrible . . . *thing* to get laid?" Now that she's dropped her arms, you can see she has the red foot in her hand. "You think you needed *this* to fuck a whore?"

"Give it back, Jade." Just looking at it makes you feel powerful again. Once you get it back, you'll be able to convince her that nothing really happened last night.

"You want it back? I'll give it back." She hops over your pants and slaps you across the face with the foot in her hand, hard. It drops to the floor. "Take it. Make love to it, for all I care. But don't you ever come looking for me again."

You think about chasing after her, but your cheek stings and the foot . . . you pick up the foot and by the time you run back to the door, she's gone. Must've been picked up by one of her older friends. You really *don't* know much about her, do you, and you're not sure if you'll be able to recover from this blunder.

You go to the shower, anticipating a little release before you hit the sack, and see blood dripping down your cheek. You don't know if the scratches are from her nails or the rabbit's, but hey, they'll give you a story to tell tomorrow.

* * *

You put a baggie of ice on your pillow and rest your cheek on it. Your skin is red and puffy around the scratches. Oh well. Maybe you'll experience a miracle like Mickey did and wake up with no marks. But then, you won't have a story to tell.

When you finally fall asleep, you have a horrible dream.

Tiny children are climbing all over you, their snot sticking to your clothes, your hands, your face, and then they turn into tiny black kittens, and they're cute for a moment until they morph into fat, red rabbits. The rabbits start nibbling on your clothes, your hair, your belly, and you start to get aroused but you know that's wrong because they're just little kids. But they're not. And they're hurting you. Their lips are full and pink and they're biting you, drawing blood. You push them off of you and run away, but you stumble over piles of rusted beer cans and fall.

You struggle to stand, but your left foot is stuck in quicksand and you can't get it out. You scream for help and see Bucky in the distance. Bucky will save you! But what? What the hell is he doing? You see his crazy right eye magnified grotesquely by the scope and he's looking right at you. No, Bucky, NO!

CHAPTER 8

YOU WAKE UP on your big day, your seventeenth birthday, and know you're not going to make it to school. Unless your iPhone is wrong, it's noon already. There are three messages from Bucky, none from Jade. You try to remember if you gave Bunny your phone number—you know your time together wore her out too— but you don't think you did. You definitely weren't thinking clearly that night.

You can't remember your dreams, but you're pretty sure they weren't wet and you don't feel rested at all. Your nose itches. Everything itches. You wonder about Bunny. After all, it's not like you asked to see her medical records before slamming her over, and over, and over.

You listen to Bucky's messages and they're all about where you are and why you're not at school. The last one's funny. It's Bucky singing his version of the birthday song, a tradition he started when you were ten.

"Happy Birthday to you, Happy Birthday TOOO you, Happy BIRTHday dear asshole, Happy Birthday to you." You hear him chuckle a little, and you remember how wicked you both thought you were by calling each other "asshole" before any other boy had the nerve to say it out loud.

You laugh, but your cheek stings like a mother. So much for your miracle. You listen to the rest of the message.

"Dude, you keep telling me sac up, so I'm giving the same advice to you. You can't skip school just to avoid dealing with Jade. Sooner or later you're gonna have to talk to her about what happened in the club. Or not. Your choice. Anyway, see you tonight at the cemetery. Let's make it eleven, OOOooooooo, that was my scary ghost imitation. And hey, it'll probably be just the two of us— people are still taking Jade's side on this one—so bring beer and we'll howl at the moon. I love you, man, even though you're a douche."

So he doesn't know about your encounter with Jade last night. Just as well.

The phone rings again, and the caller ID is from the hospital. It's the call you've been waiting for, but you don't want to talk to anyone. You feel bad enough you haven't been by to see your Gram since the freaky incident with Jade's visit. You let it go to voicemail. It's not like there's anything you can do about it today. Figures she'd die on your birthday.

"Ah, Mr. McCloud, we're calling to inform you that your grandmother is gone. Please contact us at your earliest convenience."

Goodbye, Gram, you did the best you could.

She's gone. Gone like your childhood. Gone like the parents you can't even remember anymore. Gone like your relationship with a beautiful girl. Gone like your desire to even roll out of bed today. But you've got to at least take a leak before going back to bed.

Your cheek looks horrible, all puffy, and what are those? You've been working on your facial hair, but those don't look right, and you know those hairs don't grow *that* fast. Whatever. You take a leak and fall back into bed. You really don't feel good. You'll rest up today and be ready to shoot the shit with Bucky tonight. You're glad he's your friend. Maybe you'll give *him* a birthday gift tonight, kinda make up for being such a dick all these years. Well, you'll loan it to him for a few days. He deserves to get laid too, and the foot will help him get over his insecurities.

Yes, you'll give him your foot tonight. After all, if he hadn't found it, you sure wouldn't have, and you'd never have had all the luck you've had this past week. You leave a message on his phone that you're loaning him your lucky charm tonight to make up for all the times you've been a dick-weed to him. That'll make him laugh. You set your alarm for ten p.m. No need getting there any earlier than you need to, and you sure do need the sleep.

It seems like your alarm goes off before you've even had a good nap, but sure enough, it's ten p.m., and you don't remember anything since you took a wiz. A cold beer will put you in a better frame of mind, and you'll toast your Gram, may she rest in peace.

You grab the foot from your nightstand, roll out of bed and pick your pants off the floor, but when you look down to step into them, you're horrified by what you see. Your left leg, the first one into your pants, is deformed and covered in fur. It goes numb and you fall to the floor when your foot hits the ground.

You're confused, panicked, and how the hell did your pants get over your head? You struggle, finally escaping from the smelly crotch of your pants, and you try to hop away, but your left hind leg is lame.

Hop? You're trying to hop? Your left *hind* leg is numb? None of this makes any sense to you. It's your birthday and your friend is waiting for you in the cemetery. Good thing it's right behind your house. You won't have to hop far. Good thing, too, since one of your hoppers is lame.

It takes you longer than expected to get to the cemetery, but you're okay with that. Everything's okay. Your senses are heightened and you hear Bucky talking with Jade. Oh! Good! Jade is here. But that doesn't make any sense. She hates you. Told you she was done with you. Done. Gone. Gone like Gram.

It's really dark, but you can see *McCloud* on the tombstone in front of you. You're surprised they were able to make it so quickly. When you hop closer, though, you see it's not for Gram. You read:

Wherever You Are
Aeron McCloud
RIP
Friday, November 13, 1998—
Friday, November 13, 2015

But that doesn't make any sense. That's you, and that's today, and you're still alive. Bucky and Jade can't see it. They're on the other side. You better warn them about this mistake or they might freak out. You hear Jade tell Bucky she's going to your house to give you a piece of her mind, and Bucky tells her you're not so bad. Maybe she should give you another chance. Everyone makes mistakes.

What a guy. What a pal. You better hurry before Jade sees what's chiseled on this stone.

"Bucky, look out, a rabid rabbit!" She leaps behind Bucky when she sees you hopping toward them. You laugh, but no sound comes out. You can see how she'd think that, with the way you're hopping all crooked because of your lame foot.

Oh! Good! Bucky has your rifle.

"No! Please don't do it until I leave," you hear Jade tell him. "I'll think about what you said, okay? But there's no way he's getting a birthday kiss from me tonight." You watch her make a far circle around you before running to your house.

Bucky watches her too, and when he can't see her anymore, you hear him whisper, "This one's for you, dude." You see his squinty eye from the other side of the scope and it all becomes clear to you. His aim is good. He closes both eyes when he shoots.

You feel the pain when you fall and watch your blood pump from your dying body. You watch it as it saturates the beautiful fur on your lame leg. You wonder why you're not dead yet.

Bucky approaches you slowly, and before he reaches you, he hurls. His first kill, and he doesn't even know it's you. You see him pull out a butcher's knife and can't imagine what he's going to do with it. It's clear, though, when he lays your limp body atop your own tombstone and with one brutal chop, severs your bloody hind foot from your body. The rest of the body he flings far into the woods beyond the graveyard.

So why can you still hear him?

"Hoppy Birthday, dick-weed." He chuckles at his lame pun and sticks your foot in his pocket. "Now you won't have to lend me yours."

CHAPTER 9

WHAT'S TAKING THEM so long," you hear him say. He sounds a little muffled, but you *are* in his pocket. You sense he's moving now, probably heading to your house. He stops for a moment, he's hesitating. Oh, yeah. He's thinking he might walk in on a make-up make-out session. That's funny, because you're not even there.

This should be good, you think. He's moving again, slowly, maybe listening for bedroom sounds, but you know he won't hear anything. But wait! What's that? Sobbing? Bucky's running now. You feel his dick bumping against you with each awkward stride. Gross.

You left the back door open and he runs right in, doesn't even knock or anything. Would've done that anyway, like he's always done. This is his home away from home, his escape from doting parents. Gram always treated him as good as you. Better, even. He was always so freakin' sweet to her.

"Oh, Bucky, it's horrible! Look!"

What's so horrible? What's she crying about? Your room's messy, sure, but it's not worth crying over. You hear a rustle of paper.

"Dear Gram and Bucky." Oh, he's reading a letter. You wonder who wrote it. Who'd be leaving a letter to them in your bedroom? *"You've both been the best people a person could ever want, and I've been nothing but horrible to you my whole life. I did something I'm ashamed of this week, something you know about, Bucky (please don't share), and I just can't live with it."*

What the—the letter's taking about you. It sounds like the letter's from you. But you didn't write a letter last night. Hell, you've never written a letter to anyone in your life.

"I can't live anymore with the person I've become. Please don't bother looking for me. You won't find me. I've made sure of that."

Is Bucky . . . crying? Oh, dude, don't be doing that in front of Jade. Don't be doing that in front of *anyone.*

"And whatever you do, don't blame yourselves. Don't blame anyone but me. I'm with mom and dad now, where I should have been many years ago, so be happy for me. I love you both for everything you've ever done for me. Waiting for you in Heaven, Aeron."

Waiting for you in Heaven? As if you'd actually ever say something like that. There's no way Bucky will believe this letter's from you. What the hell's going on here?

"Oh, Bucky, what are we going to do?" Jade is crying again, and you can feel her, you can *smell* her heat through Bucky's pocket. Is she hugging him? You feel a kind of bouncing and hear them both crying. Yup. They're hugging each other and crying together. How sweet. How—wait a minute. What. Is. Going. On. Here.

It seems like they're never going to stop crying, but they finally do.

"On his birthday." Bucky sounds defeated. You want to scream, *"Sac up, bro! I'm right here!"* but you can't. You can't do anything but listen and feel and smell—God, Bucky! You couldn't have put on clean boxers for my party?—and wonder what the hell you're doing trapped in a bloody rabbit's foot in your best friend's pocket.

"I feel horrible, Bucky. I bet he never really even cheated on me. I should've gone to school that day. I should've talked to him instead of listening to all those nasty rumors."

What? Wait. She talked to you. She knows. You wonder what Bucky will say now. He knows too.

"It's not your fault, Jade. Maybe he was drugged. He'd never do something to purposely hurt you, I know that. He really did love you."

Yup, that's Bucky for you. Always taking the high road. Always has your back. You feel like giggling again because now he has your foot.

"I didn't even date him for that long, but I thought maybe he could be the one, you know? Maybe we should drink one for Aeron. He was pretty psyched about getting us beers for his party, remember? I think he'd want that."

"Yeah. You're right. Be right back." You feel Bucky walking again and hear the fridge open. He's grabbing a cold six-pack and bringing it back to the bedroom. You wish you could down one right now. It's all stuffy and crotchy in there.

You hear the pop and the fizz.

"To Aeron," Jade says, but she sounds sad.

"To Aeron," Bucky says, and you're glad he doesn't add dick-wad or dick-weed or asshole or any of the other nasty names you call one another.

You hear them smack their lips after the first chug and you feel Bucky suppressing a burp. How do you know that?

"I know this might sound insensitive, Bucky, but we might as well make this a party, right? A celebration of his life? I'm pretty sure he got chips and things for tonight."

"Yeah. I can hear him right now telling me to—"

You know he won't say "sac up" in front of Jade, but you wish he would.

"—anyway, yeah. Be right back." Off to the kitchen again for chips.

Too bad you can't see what Jade's putting in Bucky's beer right now. Maybe there'd be a way to stop him from drinking it.

It doesn't take long before Bucky's beer is gone. You didn't hear much crunching, so they probably didn't even eat many chips. What a waste. You start to feel weird, as if being a rabbit's foot in your best friend's pants pocket isn't weird enough.

"Hey, Jade, don't cry again. It's breaking my heart to see you so sad. Come here." Bucky's holding her now. You can smell her again, so close. He's rubbing her back and you feel the tickle of cashmere. You have no idea how, but hey, it feels good. A wave of dizziness hits you. Bucky's heart rate is going crazy and he's sweating, his breathing's shallow.

You feel her arms around him, her hands searching for something—AHH! She's found you! She's caressing you through his pocket! You can feel something growing, pressing against you, squeezing you in the confines of his pocket. Oh, fuck no! You're so dizzy now, her words sound like they're coming from inside a tunnel, a hot, wet tunnel—

"Ooo, Bucky, it's so stiff! Come on, baby, comfort me."

You hear the sound of a zipper and the creaking of your bedsprings as you're smashed again and again between Bucky's thigh and your crusty mattress. It's over quickly, and you feel his weight heavy between Jade's legs. You feel his hands sliding beneath her, holding her bottom tightly while he's still inside her.

"Whoa, is that a ta—"

No! Hang on, Bucky! Hang on! But then, lights out.

---

* * *

The sound of your front door opening is far, far away. Bucky can't move. You wish he'd roll over and give you some space.

"He was quick. Quick like a bunny, just the way I like it," you hear Jade tell someone, and then you hear the familiar laughter of another woman.

"One of these will be the one, I can feel it. Here, feel my belly."

You sense Bucky's drugged confusion. You don't even understand what's happening.

"Yes! I think you're right!" the woman says, and now you know. "Probably five or six! One of these little red-headed kittens will surely be the one, and then we'll never have to worry about getting shot at again. He'll make sure of that."

What the hell is Bunny doing in your bedroom?

"Thanks again for testing him," Jade says. "You've had to take a lot for the herd."

"Yes, but you know me, sweetie. I may be too old to breed them, but I'm never too old to enjoy a little nibble now and then, and that last one filled me up *full*! I know you liked him, but even Gram knew he wasn't the one. Speak of the devil, here she is now."

But . . . but . . . Gram's gone! What are they talking about? And WHAT, THE, HELL is going on here?

"Hey, Gram. Right on the stroke of midnight. Good to get you back." Jade speaks to someone, but it can't be Gram, and you hear a throaty *purrrrrrrr*. "It must've been tough spending all those years raising someone you knew wasn't the one."

Bunny says she can't understand how the foot could be so wrong. The one who found it was supposed to be *the one*.

"I guess we're lucky it ended up being his best friend. Pure, sweet Bucky."

It sounds like they don't bother closing the door when they leave because you can hear them leaping away.

* * *

Bucky will wake up in a puddle of drool on your pillow and wonder why he's there, and why his pants are halfway off. He'll read your letter again—Jade's letter—and cry for a few more minutes before drying his eyes and going home for comfort from his mom.

Kids at school will wonder what happened to Jade, but they'll forget about her a day later. New kids often just disappear. No big thing. She never really did fit in, and no one ever met her parents. Some of the girls will cry when they hear about your letter. Local police will investigate your disappearance, but they'll find no leads. The hospital will keep hush about losing one of their patients, and with no family to question, they'll return to business as usual.

Bucky will keep your foot forever in remembrance of you and your last hunting trip together. He'll wish you could have seen him shoot the "rabid rabbit" in the cemetery on your birthday. He thinks the foot is disgusting, but it makes him laugh. It makes him feel like a man for some reason, though he doesn't know why. And he doesn't know why he feels the need to keep it with him wherever he goes.

You know why. And for the next several years, maybe even decades, you'll feel/smell/hear everything Bucky does because you'll be right there in his pocket. You'll be his lucky charm. Someday, someone else will find your nasty old foot behind a trunk in an old garage and set you free.

It's not your fault, really. You couldn't have known. You were just a horny teenage jerk like every other horny teenage jerk. All you really wanted was to get fucked.

And now, well, you are.

THE END

Acknowledgments

"Let's do the 3-Day Novel Contest," my friend Stephanie Stroh suggested one summer day. She's the one who announced to our writing group a few years back: "I'm doing NaNoWriMo this year. Who's going to join me?" Thus, I credit her with inspiring me to try my hand at yet another crazy writing challenge.

Sincere thanks to my lustful house muse. You took my initial idea for this story and somehow made me write something quite different. Not sure I could have done this without you. Keep it up, please.

From the very center of my heart, I thank my ever-more-encouraging-each-year husband, Mike, for leaving Stephanie and me alone that entire Labor Day Weekend to write like wackadoodles, and for giving me two thumbs up after reading this naughty tale. Did I mention he may have been heavily sedated while awaiting surgery? I'm certain it didn't affect his judgment.

About the Author

LAUREL McHARGUE was raised in Braintree, Massachusetts, but somehow found her way to the breathtaking elevation of Colorado's Rocky Mountains, where she has taught and currently lives and laughs and writes and podcasts.

She hosts the weekly podcast *Alligator Preserves* and also has been known to act. Visit Laurel on her blog where she writes and narrates stories about life, real and imagined.

www.leadvillelaurel.com

A Personal Note from Laurel

I would love to hear from you! I'm serious about
the "visit me in Leadville" comment, but until you
might make that happen, connect with me here:

Facebook: Leadville Laurel (author page)
Twitter: @LeadvilleLaurel
LinkedIn: Laurel (Bernier) McHargue
Web Page: www.leadvillelaurel.com
Email: laurel.mchargue@gmail.com
Podcast:
https://soundcloud.com/laurelmchargue

Check out my other publications on Amazon and
let me know what you think!

And remember, we struggling
authors/musicians/artists/actors love positive
feedback, so if you like what we do, please consider
writing reviews of our work! If you don't like what
we do, well, if you can't say something nice . . .